RUBY IN THE RUINS

For Tom and Celia,
with love and gratitude

First published 2018 by Walker Books Ltd 87 Vauxhall Walk, London SE11 5HJ • 2 4 6 8 10 9 7 5 3 1
© 2018 Shirley Hughes • The right of Shirley Hughes to be identified as author/illustrator of this
work has been asserted by her in accordance with the Copyright, Designs and Patents Act 1988
This book has been typeset in Futura T • Printed in China • All rights reserved. No part of this
book may be reproduced, transmitted or stored in an information retrieval system in any form or by
any means, graphic, electronic or mechanical, including photocopying, taping and
recording, without prior written permission from the publisher • British Library Cataloguing
in Publication Data: a catalogue record for this book is available from the British Library
ISBN 978-1-4063-7589-3 • www.walker.co.uk

RUBY IN THE RUINS

Shirley Hughes

WALKER BOOKS
AND SUBSIDIARIES
LONDON • BOSTON • SYDNEY • AUCKLAND

1945 WORLD WAR II WAS OVER!

The fighting had ended and peace had come at last. Bombs no longer fell on London, but many houses on the streets near where Ruby and her mum lived were in ruins, with blackened, burnt-out roofs. Men were already at work there, clearing up the rubble.

DANGER

KEEP OUT!

MINISTRY OF
DEFENCE

Ruby's dad was a soldier, still serving far away abroad. Many of their neighbours had been evacuated to live safely in the country during the Blitz, but Mum had refused to budge.

"We must be here for Dad in case he gets leave," she said. "I'm not having him come home unexpectedly to find an empty house."

Ruby had been sent away to a safe area with the other children from her school, but in the end she was so homesick that she had come home to Mum.

Every night when the warning sirens wailed and searchlights swept the sky, they had awaited the menacing drone of approaching enemy bombers.

Then came the terrifying explosions, some quite nearby,
making their little terrace house shake.
Mum hated going down to the cold,
crowded, smelly air raid shelter.

So, night after night, she and Ruby
clung together in the big double bed,
blocking their ears and praying
for the All-Clear to sound
at dawn.

At last, the joyful day of victory arrived! Union Jack flags flew everywhere. All the neighbours who were still in residence pooled their rations to have a glorious street party. The children sat at long tables and tucked in to the delicious sandwiches, cake and even chocolate biscuits!

Len Parker's dad was the first to come home.
The whole street turned out to greet him.

Then Jimmy Nolan's dad,
who was a sailor, turned up
on an extended leave.

But Ruby and Mum had to wait
a long time until, at last, the great day
arrived when they set out to the
station to meet Dad.

It was very crowded.

Ruby hardly recognized the big sunburned man
who got off the train with all the other soldiers,
shouldering his heavy kit bag and waving to them.

Mum ran forward and flung herself into his arms.
Ruby hung back, feeling very shy. She did not
know what to say when he stooped down
to kiss her.

From then on, everything at home changed.

 Ruby had to move into the little bedroom in the attic.

Mum promised that they would re-decorate it as soon as they could,

but at the moment it was very draughty and shabby.

 A lot of plaster had fallen off the ceiling during the Blitz,

and once or twice Ruby thought she heard a mouse

scuttle across the floor.

Dad had been promised his old job back, although he had not yet started work.
Ruby had forgotten how very big he was, and what a lot of space he took up,
sitting about in their little kitchen.

Sometimes Ruby and her friends would talk about their dads.

"My dad goes out a lot," Len Parker told her. "He wants to meet up with his old army buddies and talk about the war and stuff."

"So does mine," said Jimmy. "Len and I like to go exploring sometimes. You can come with us if you like."

"I'm not sure my mum'll let me," said Ruby.

In the end she pleaded so hard that Mum
gave in. "Well all right love," she said.
"Just so long as you don't go far away.
Stay around the neighbourhood,
and take care!"

What Mum didn't know was that Jimmy and Len loved playing on bomb sites. These were supposed to be fenced off, but it was easy to find a way through the wire.

These forbidden places were
full of rubble and fallen beams,
and flights of stairs leading
to nowhere.

The children loved this wonderful playground.
Len and Jimmy climbed all over the wreckage
like mountain goats, not caring how very dangerous it was.

Ruby soon became as adventurous
as they were. She slid over piles of rubble,
see-sawed on fallen rafters and stood on tiptoe
on half-destroyed walls to view the ruins all around.

But one day when they were playing there a very bad thing happened. Ruby made an extra big jump across a fallen rafter, missed her footing and fell.

Jimmy and Len stopped playing at once and ran to help her.

Ruby's knee was badly grazed and she did not want to get up.

She started to cry.

"You'd better run back to her house and fetch her mum!" said Len.

"Quick as you can, Jimmy! I'll stay here with her."

Ruby lay there for what seemed like hours. Len tried to cheer her up,
but she just closed her eyes.

Then she felt a pair of strong arms around her.

Not Mum's arms. Not Jimmy or Len's arms. It was her dad!

"Don't worry, love. We'll have you out of here in no time!" he said.

When they got home, Dad bathed her leg and
put a bandage on it. Ruby managed not to cry.
Afterwards she sat beside him on the sofa,
eating a biscuit. He wasn't a bit cross about
her playing in the rubble.

   "You're an adventurous one!" he said.
"And so are those two lads,
Jimmy and Len. A couple of troopers!
I should give those bomb sites
a miss and play in the
park from now on
if I were you!"

"Oh, Dad, I'm so glad you're back!" was all Ruby could say.
And for the first time since he had come home,
she put her arms around his neck and kissed him.

YOUR RATION BOOK

ISSUED

TO SAFEGUARD

YOUR FOOD SUPPLY

JOHNSON

IN CASE OF AN

AIR RAID

GO INTO YOUR SHELTER
AND STAY THERE.
TAKE GAS MASK
WITH YOU ALSO

SHELTER BEDS

RECIPES FOR 26 DIFFERENT KINDS OF SANDWICHES, MADE ENTIRELY WITHOUT BUTTER

KEEP UP THE PAPER CHASE!

Waste paper is a vital necessity for supplying munitions for our world wide battlefronts. Every home can help to keep up the supply.

Take it from me

Rubber soles and heels double the life of your shoes

MAKE LAST YEAR'S CLOTHES LAST YEARS